First published 1992 by Walker Books Ltd
87 Vauxhall Walk, London SE11 5HJ

This edition published 2009

2 4 6 8 10 9 7 5 3 1

© 1992 Lucy Su

The right of Lucy Su to be identified as author/illustrator of this work
has been asserted by her in accordance with the Copyright, Designs and Patents Act 1988

This book has been typeset in Garamond Educational

Printed in China

British Library Cataloguing in Publication Data:
a catalogue record for this book is available from the British Library.

ISBN 978-0-7445-2223-5

www.walker.co.uk

Jinzi and Minzi are Friends

Lucy Su

WALKER BOOKS
AND SUBSIDIARIES
LONDON · BOSTON · SYDNEY · AUCKLAND

Jinzi and Minzi are friends.

Jinzi likes dolls,
Minzi likes panda bears.

Jinzi likes dancing,
Minzi likes singing.

Jinzi likes cars,
Minzi likes zebras.

Jinzi likes strawberries,
Minzi likes blackberries.

Jinzi and Minzi both like hats.

But Jinzi likes spots
and Minzi likes stripes.

That's better!